En Mi CaSa y En La EScuela

by
Angelita Valdez, LMSW, RPT-S
and Marisela Sierra

AuthorHouse™
1663 Liberty Drive
Bloomington, IN 47403
www.authorhouse.com
Phone: 833-262-8899

Because of the dynamic nature of the Internet, any web addresses or links contained in this
book may have changed since publication and may no longer be valid. The views expressed
in this work are solely those of the authors and do not necessarily reflect the views of
the publisher, and the publisher hereby disclaims any responsibility for them.

Any people depicted in stock imagery provided by Getty Images are models,
and such images are being used for illustrative purposes only.
Certain stock imagery © Getty Images.

This book is printed on acid-free paper.

ISBN: 978-1-6655-6986-6 (sc)
ISBN: 978-1-6655-6987-3 (e)

Library of Congress Control Number: 2022916452

Print information available on the last page.

Published by AuthorHouse 09/08/2022

authorHOUSE®

Dedication

Para Nana y Abuela: Thank you for teaching us to be proud of who we are and to embrace our roots.

Para Matias y Vivianna: remember to be proud of who you are and to love both worlds that you live in.

Hola, me llamo Felix. Hi, my name is Anna. We are special because we live in two worlds. *En mi casa* we are able to spend time with our *familia* and *en la escuela* we are able to spend time with our friends and teacher.

En mi casa we say "*Buenos Días*," *en la escuela* we say "Good Morning."

En mi casa we eat *pan dulce, en la escuela* we eat pancakes.

4

En mi casa we play *fútbol, en la escuela* we play soccer at recess.

6

En mi casa we listen to salsa music, *en la escuela* we play instruments in music class.

8

En mi casa abuela tells us *cuentos, en la escuela* we read books at story time.

En mi casa we eat *tortas, en la escuela* we eat sandwiches at lunch.

En mi casa we *respetar a nuestros mayores, en la escuela* we listen to our teachers.

En mi casa we give *besitos* to our family, *en la escuela* we give high fives to our friends.

En mi casa we say *"Hasta Mañana,"* en *la escuela* we say "See You Tomorrow."

What are three things you do in your casa?

En mi casa.............

En mi casa.............

En mi casa.............

What are three things you do in *la escuela?*

En la escuela..........

En la escuela..........

En la escuela..........

Printed in the United States
by Baker & Taylor Publisher Services